ALLOSAURUS

CORYTHOSAURUS

PTERANODON

APATOSAURUS

DIMETRODON

ANKYLOSAURUS

TRACHODON

TYRANNOSAURUS REX

STEGOSAURUS

TRICERATOPS

ALLOSAURUS

CORYTHOSAURUS

PTERANODON

APATOSAURUS

DIMETRODON

ANKYLOSAURUS

TRACHODON

TYRANNOSAURUS REX

STEGOSAURUS

TRICERATOPS

JANE YOLEN

How Do Dinosaurs

Say Good Night?

Illustrated by

MARK TEAGUE

Scholastic Inc. · New York

This book was originally published in hardcover by The Blue Sky Press in 2000.

ISBN 978-1-338-74491-0

Text copyright © 2000 by Jane Yolen
Illustrations copyright © 2000 by Mark Teague
All rights reserved. Published by Scholastic Inc.,
Publishers since 1920. SCHOLASTIC and associated logos are
trademarks and/or registered trademarks of Scholastic Inc.

The publisher does not have any control over and does not assume any
responsibility for author or third-party websites or their content.

12 11 10 9 8 7 6 5 4 3 2   21 22 23 24 25

Printed in the U.S.A.   40

This edition first printing, May 2021

The final artwork was done in acrylic paints.

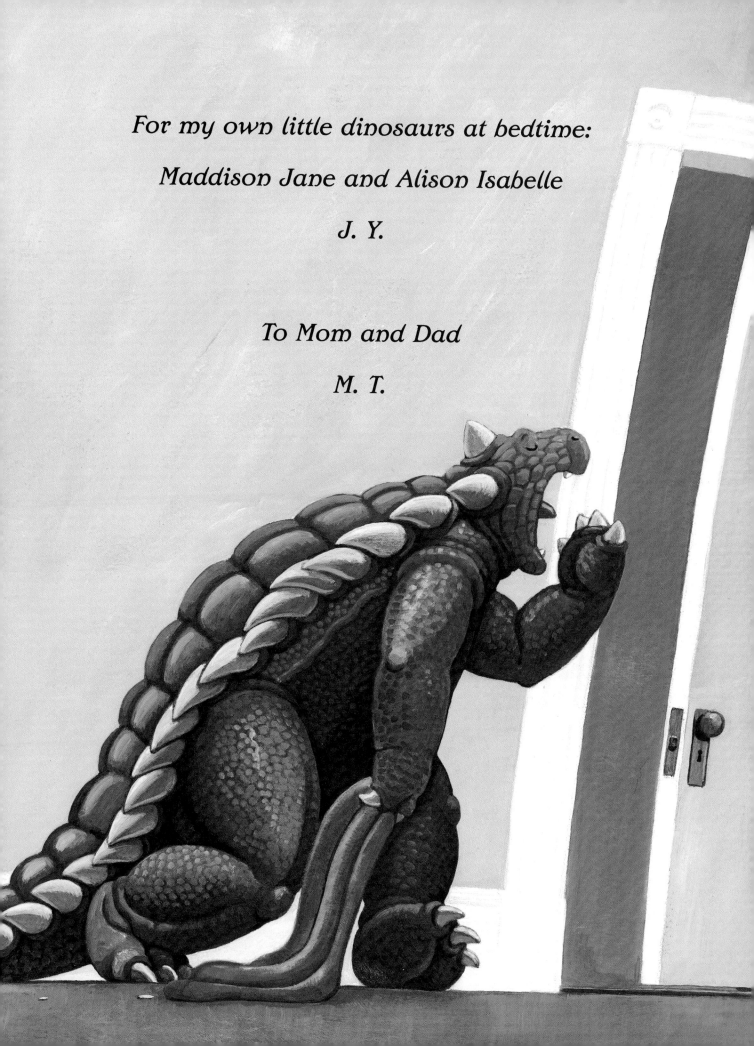

For my own little dinosaurs at bedtime:
Maddison Jane and Alison Isabelle

J. Y.

To Mom and Dad

M. T.

How does
a dinosaur say
good night
when Papa
comes in
to turn off
the light?

Does
a dinosaur
slam
his tail
and pout?

Does he throw
his teddy bear
all about?

Does a
dinosaur
stomp
his feet
on the floor

and shout:
"I want
to hear
one book
more!"?

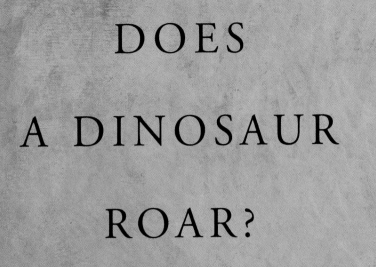

DOES

A DINOSAUR

ROAR?

How does a dinosaur say good night
when *Mama* comes in
to turn off the light?

Does he swing his neck

from side to side?

Does he up
and demand
a piggyback ride?

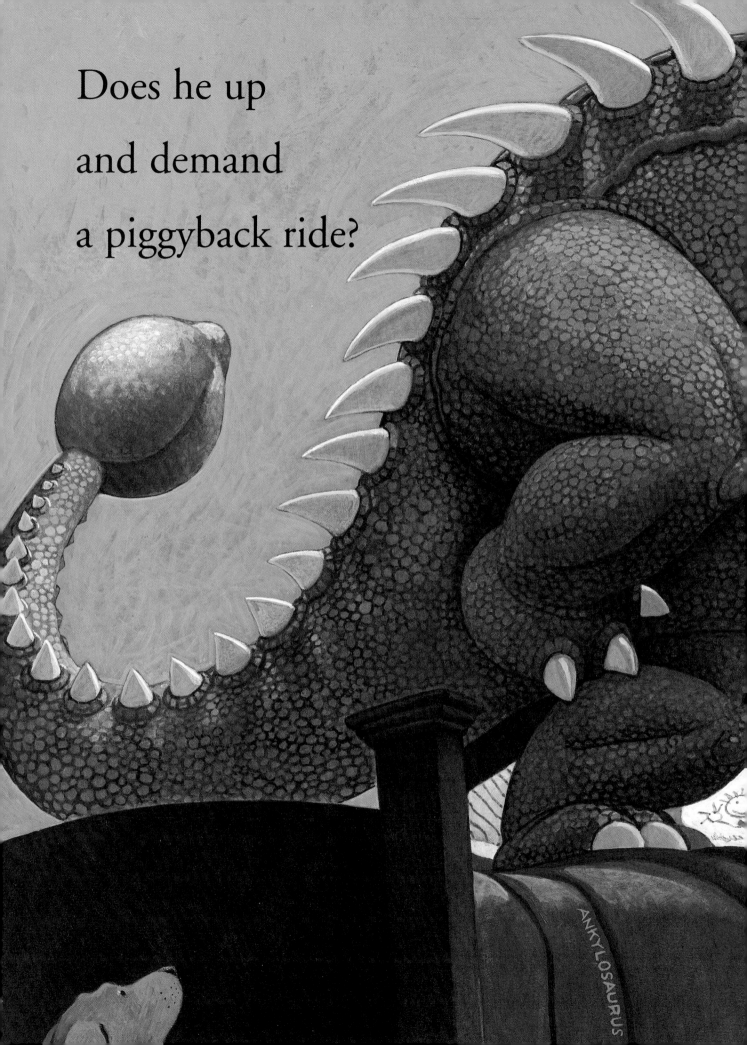

Does he mope,
does he moan,
does he sulk,
does he sigh?

Does he fall on the top
of his covers and cry?

No, dinosaurs don't.
They don't even try.

They give
a big kiss.

STEGOSAURUS

They turn out
the light.

They tuck in
their tails.
They whisper,
"Good night!"

They give
a big hug,
then give
one kiss
more.

Good night.

Good night, little dinosaur.

ALLOSAURUS

PTERANODON

CORYTHOSAURUS

APATOSAURUS

DIMETRODON

ANKYLOSAURUS

TRACHODON

TYRANNOSAURUS REX

STEGOSAURUS

TRICERATOPS

ALLOSAURUS

PTERANODON

CORYTHOSAURUS

APATOSAURUS

DIMETRODON

ANKYLOSAURUS

TRACHODON

TYRANNOSAURUS REX

STEGOSAURUS

TRICERATOPS